CHARLOTTE   BRANWELL

EMILY   ANNE

Text and illustrations copyright © Catherine Brighton 1994

First published in the United States of America by Chronicle Books
275 Fifth Street, San Francisco, California 94103

First published in Great Britain in 1994 by Frances Lincoln Limited
The Brontës was conceived, edited, and produced by Frances Lincoln Limited,
4 Torriano Mews, Torriano Avenue, London NW5 2RZ

CIP Data Available.
ISBN 0-8118-0608-1   33136

Printed in Hong Kong

9 8 7 6 5 4 3 2 1

The
BRONTËS

Scenes from the childhood of Charlotte,
Branwell, Emily and Anne.

Catherine Brighton

CHRONICLE BOOKS ● SAN FRANCISCO

Prologue

This book is about four extraordinary children: Charlotte, Branwell, Emily and Anne Brontë.

Over a hundred years ago, they lived in a lonely parsonage by a church in the remote village of Haworth. They never mixed with the children who lived in the village but played make-believe games together in and around the parsonage. When they were very young their mother died, and soon afterwards their two elder sisters, Maria and Elizabeth, died too.

Here Charlotte tells of their childhood on the wild northern moors.

 ## The Moors

On Mondays, Tabby the maid scrubs the flagstones and we are forbidden to enter until they are clean and dry.

Papa hurries us into our coats and hats and we follow him happily out onto the moors. Haworth moors are the biggest and best back garden in the world. Emily carries her hawk on her gauntlet, and the dog runs on ahead.

It is Papa's time for teaching us about God. He waves his arms wide
to show God's generosity.

We examine lepidoptera and the calices of flowers with a spy glass,
and we study geography and astronomy using Papa's telescope. On our
way home, we sing hymns as loud as we can. God surely must hear our
voices echoing through the darkening hills.

The Great Bogburst

It is September and we are exploring a gully.

Suddenly a storm breaks above us. Lightning fires its arrows into the ground, and the rain comes down so hard that rivers and rocks tumble down the steep hillside. The ground opens before our feet, and explosions of mud and rocks shoot up in the air.

"It's wonderful!" shouts Emily from a high rock. "It's an earthquake."

At home, dear Papa cannot work. He stands at the lighted window, anxiously waiting and praying for our safe return.

Later, when we are huddled safely around the fire, Aunt Branwell wraps us in blankets. "Truly," I say to Papa, "it was exciting to see the world like it is in the Bible pictures."

The Forbidden Games

Papa has gone to Leeds, and while he is away we play noisy forbidden games. We slide down the banisters, shout as much as we can, and let Emily's geese into the house. Tabby chases us out into the garden with her broom.

We escape her by climbing Papa's double cherry tree and sit on the branches like roosting birds. As dusk falls over Haworth, we creep inside again for our bread and milk.

 # The Young Men

The morning after Papa's return from Leeds, Branwell comes to our
bedroom door. He is clutching a red wooden box.

"Look what Papa has brought me. Soldiers!"

"Let's see," I cry. Branwell opens the box and I snatch up a soldier.

"This one shall be mine!" I cry. Emily and Anne do the same.

We sit holding our soldiers like precious statues until Branwell says, "Let's play battles!"

So we do, and we call our soldiers the Young Men.

The Battles

Since the Young Men have arrived, our playtime has become far more exciting. Branwell invents famous battle games, and our soldiers are all generals.

Mine is the Duke of Wellington, Emily's is called Gravey because he looks serious and grave, Anne calls hers Waiting Boy (I don't know why), and Branwell has Napoleon Bonaparte, so he can have good battles with me.

Sometimes our battles last all day, and everyone is dead by the evening. We have invented a rule called *making alive* so the game can continue the next day.

The Imagination

Sometimes we make up stories about a fantastic new city, the Great Glass Town Confederacy. We, the Four Genii (we've been reading the *Arabian Nights*), are its rulers and generals.

At night I stand at the window going over in my mind what the Duke of Wellington will do tomorrow. The moon enlightens me.

At dawn the Duke wakes me, and I tiptoe to Papa's study. I always find the answers to my problems in books and atlases. I find the name of a new exotic country, and the Duke and I decide to be explorers and set sail for new shores.

The Meeting of the Waters

Often we take our made-up characters to our favorite place on the moors, a place we call the Meeting of the Waters. If we go for the whole day, we pretend that our belongings are the generals' luggage.

Emily, of course, brings her hawk, Anne looks after the dog, and Branwell has the Young Men in their box. We carry between us a lunch basket, fishing nets and our books. In the heat of summer it feels like foreign travel.

Out of the hazy blue, I imagine a hot air balloon emerging. It silently traverses the sky, and I climb in with the Duke. An adventure follows, and we are back before Emily has unpacked lunch. What bliss.

The Mask

On Sunday evening, Papa calls us to his study, and we sit in a line on the sofa.

His voice drones on as he reads the Holy Bible. My mind returns to the Duke of Wellington, who is in danger. I must save him.

"Charlotte! What must you do to be saved?" Papa is asking me. I have forgotten. I must save the Duke.

Then Papa, seeing we are bored, takes down the mask he keeps on

the wall. He hands it to me and I put it on. When we wear this mask, we must tell the truth.

"Where were you just now, Charlotte?" asks Papa. "Something tells me you were elsewhere."

"Yes, Papa. I was in Togoland with the Duke of Wellington."

Papa peers at me over his spectacles, takes the mask, and returns with a sigh to reading from the Holy Bible.

✂ The Books

We, the Genii, have started to write books. The secret plays and wild games are going to be written down!

We collect old envelopes and grocery bags and cut the paper into tiny sheets. The covers are made from blue sugar bags, and we sew the sides with a needle and thread.

Sometimes we cut and write, read and write, sew and write all morning, all afternoon, and until the candles gutter deep into the evening.

Our writing is so tiny, and our books so very small, you can only read them with a magnifying glass.

The Dream

One winter evening, Emily plays the piano while Anne reads and
Branwell writes his little books. The dog is blinking at the flames.
I sit atop Papa's ladder and look out of the window to where the moors
are blanketed in snow.

When the snow stops falling, I can see Glass Town emerging in my mind. I see the Duke of Wellington pass by on his horse and the moon moving in and out of the clouds.

I think that one day I would like to become a real writer.

Epilogue

The Four Genii continued to produce tiny books and to create fantasy-lands. Their writing and imaginings turned first into poetry and later on into novels. Branwell tried unsuccessfully to become a writer and painter.

Sadly, they all died when they were still quite young, but they live on through their books.

Charlotte's best-known book is *Jane Eyre*, Emily's is *Wuthering Heights* and Anne's *The Tenant of Wildfell Hall*. Many of their ideas came from their childhood experiences and surroundings, and play an important part in the history of English literature.

CHARLOTTE   **BRANWELL**

EMILY   **ANNE**